The Princess and the Pea

and other stories

Miles Kelly

First published in 2011 by Miles Kelly Publishing Ltd
Harding's Barn, Bardfield End Green, Thaxted, Essex, CM6 3PX, UK

Copyright © Miles Kelly Publishing Ltd 2011

This edition printed 2013

2 4 6 8 10 9 7 5 3

Publishing Director Belinda Gallagher
Creative Director Jo Cowan
Editor Amanda Askew
Senior Designer Joe Jones
Designer Kayleigh Allen
Production Manager Elizabeth Collins
Reprographics Anthony Cambray, Stephan Davis, Jennifer Hunt
Assets Lorraine King

ISBN 978-1-84810-435-8

Printed in China

British Library Cataloguing-in-Publication Data
A catalogue record for this book is available from the British Library

ACKNOWLEDGEMENTS
Artworks are from the Miles Kelly Artwork Bank

Made with paper from a sustainable forest

www.mileskelly.net
info@mileskelly.net
www.factsforprojects.com

Contents

The Seven Ravens

A Polish fairytale

There was once a poor widow who had seven sons and a daughter. The daughter, Anne, was a good girl, but the seven brothers were wild as the hills. One day the widow was baking a pie. As she rolled out the pastry the noisy troop came into the kitchen shouting, "Pie! When will it be ready?"

"When it is cooked," she said crossly. "Let me finish then we can all eat." But the boys just ran about the hot kitchen, pushing and shoving and leaving muddy bootmarks all over the floor.

"Quiet! I wish you were ravens instead of noisy boys," she cried. Her eyes widened in horror — the boys shrank, feathers covered them, their mouths became beaks, and they flew out of the door. Anne rushed to the window, but they were already out of sight. Mother and daughter sat weeping, and not even the smell of burning pie could rouse them.

The next day Anne told her mother that she would find her brothers and bring them home.

She set off with nothing but her needle, thread and scissors. She walked until she came to a strange house in the woods. It was made of silver, and the woman who opened the door was dressed in a long silver robe. "Oh, my husband will be home soon. There is no supper ready, and I have to mend his cloak," she said all in a rush.

"I could mend the cloak," said Anne taking out her needle, "and then you can cook the supper."

The woman was delighted and let her in. Anne sat in the corner and mended the beautiful cloak with the tiny stitches. When the husband came in, also dressed in silver, he invited Anne to join them for a supper of roast chicken.

The silver man asked Anne where she was going so she told them the whole story of her brothers.

"We are the moon's helpers," said the silver man. "I will ask her if she has seen your brothers."

As the wife cleared the table after supper, she gave Anne the chicken bones and said, "Keep these in your pocket – they might come in useful."

When the silver man returned the next morning he told Anne that the moon had seen seven ravens flying round Amber Mountain. Anne thanked them and set off.

After several days she came to a halt at Amber Mountain. Its sides were as steep as glass. Anne remembered the chicken bones. She pushed one into the surface of the mountain and stood on it. Then she put the second bone in and stood on that, and so she slowly climbed to the top of the mountain. There she found seven ravens – her brothers! But an evil old witch was there too.

"Your brothers are under my spell. You can release them by remaining silent for seven years," and with an evil cackle she flew off.

Anne climbed down the mountain, and when

she got home she could tell her mother nothing. Four years passed until one day Anne met a prince who was struck by Anne's quiet ways. He came by every day, and asked her to marry him. She smiled her acceptance but didn't utter a word.

Three more years passed, and the prince and Anne had a baby son. Now the queen had never really approved of her son marrying such a poor girl and so she liked to make mischief. One day she accused Anne of trying to poison the baby. The prince was horrified and when he asked Anne if she had done such a terrible thing, she was unable to reply. So he sent her to the dungeons.

Three days passed and Anne was brought into the courtyard where everyone waited to see what would happen next. Suddenly there was a great flapping of wings and seven ravens landed in a circle around Anne. In a blink of an eye there stood her brothers, restored to human shape.

Well, you can imagine what a lot Anne had to tell! They talked into the night. The seven brothers went to collect their mother, and when they all came back together, the prince promised her that she would never have to do a day's work again!

The Golden Touch

A myth from ancient Greece

There was once a king called Midas who loved gold more than anything in the world. Each day, he spent hour after hour in his treasure house, running his hands through his sacks of gold coins, admiring his golden jars and statues, and holding up his golden jewellery to the light to watch it gleam and shine. Midas thought that the precious metal was a much more delightful colour than the emerald green of the grass or the sapphire blue of the sea. He thought it was far more beautiful than the gold of waving fields of wheat, the gold of his wife's hair – even the gold of sunshine.

The king once helped the god Dionysus by taking care of one of his friends who was lost. Dionysus was very grateful and insisted, "Let me repay you for your kindness by granting you a wish! Now think hard… Make it something good! Whatever you like."

Midas knew exactly what he wanted. "I wish for everything I touch to turn to gold!" he declared.

"Are you sure about that?" Dionysus asked. "Are you quite, quite sure?"

"What could be better?" cried Midas, delightedly.

"Very well then," sighed the god. "It is done."

Midas couldn't wait to try out his new powers. He hurried over to a tree and snapped off a twig.

Unbelievable! It immediately grew heavy and bright. It had turned to solid gold. Joyfully, Midas rushed around touching everything in his royal garden. Soon the apples hung on the trees like golden baubles. The flowers hardened into gold sculptures. The fountain froze into a spray of golden glitter and the grass solidified into a gold pavement. "How wonderful!" laughed Midas, clapping his hands. "Now for my palace!" and he picked up his robes and ran inside. By the time Midas reached the cool of his great chamber, his clothes had stiffened into a fabric woven from pure gold thread. "Ooof!" puffed Midas. "That's a little heavy!" The weight of his golden clothes were dragging him down, slowing him up and making his shoulders ache.

Still, thought Midas, that's a minor botheration compared to how beautiful my robes now look! He set off through the halls and corridors, touching pillars, pictures, doors, furniture, floors... until everything glowed gold.

Phew! It was hungry, thirsty work! Midas sank into one of his new golden chairs at his new golden dining table and called for his servants to bring him his lunch. He wriggled about a bit on his rock hard seat, but couldn't get comfy. "Never mind!" said Midas to himself, as the servants brought in platter after platter of delicious food. "I don't know any other king who is rich enough to eat off gold plates!" And he touched each serving dish and bowl and saw them gleam.

"Amazing!" Midas whooped, and licking his lips, he reached for a juicy chicken leg. "OWWW!" he yelled, biting down on hard metal and breaking a tooth. He reached for a goblet of wine and took a gulp. "AAARRGH!" Midas roared, as the mouthful of gold got stuck in his throat. The king pushed his chair back, spitting out the hunk of treasure.

"Oh, no!" the king moaned. Suddenly he realized what the god Dionysus had been trying to warn him about. "I'm going to have a whole kingdom full of gold, but I'm not going to be able to eat or drink anything!"

At that very moment, Midas's golden doors swung open and his little daughter came running towards him. Midas backed away in horror – but it was too late. "Daddy!" the little girl cried, flinging her arms happily around him. Suddenly the king's beloved daughter was no more than a lifeless statue. Midas howled with misery and huge tears began to stream from his eyes. "I would gladly give away every piece of gold that I own to have my little girl back again," he wailed. "How foolish I have been! There must be some way to take back my wish!"

Desperately trying not to touch anything else, Midas hurried to Dionysus and begged him to undo his magic. "Go and wash in the River Pactolus," the god instructed him. As soon as the king had done so, he was hugely relieved to find that his golden touch was gone. All the things Midas had turned into gold were back to normal – including his beautiful little daughter. After that, if the king had had his way, he would never have looked at another nugget of gold as long as he lived. But the god Dionysus turned the sandy bed of the River Pactolus gold for ever more, so that every time Midas walked along its banks, he would remember his greedy mistake.

The Sword in the Stone

A Celtic legend

The blacksmith's anvil had suddenly appeared in the courtyard of the cathedral on Christmas morning. No one knew how it had got there. The anvil had a sword stuck into it and stood on a huge stone. Words were carved right round it which read: Whoever pulls out this sword is the rightful king of the Britons.

Many a proud lord had stepped up and tried to pull the sword out of the mysterious anvil. But even though they had heaved and sweated and grunted and pulled and pulled and pulled, all of them had walked away disappointed. Now almost a week had passed. It was time for the New Year's Eve jousting festival, and still the anvil stood on the stone in the courtyard with the sword sticking out of it.

Every year, bold knights came to the capital city from all over the kingdom to ride against each other in the New Year's Eve jousting festival and show off how brave they were. This year, Sir Ector's son, Sir Kay, would joust for the very first time. Sir Ector's younger son, Arthur, was going along too, as Sir Kay's squire. Sir Ector and his sons lived in the very furthest corner of the kingdom – so far away from the capital city that news of the strange anvil hadn't even reached them. It took them three days of hard riding until they saw the towering cathedral spire and the bright fluttering flags of the jousting field in the distance. Then a dreadful thing happened. Sir Kay put his hand down by his side to pat his trusty sword – and there was nothing there. "My sword!" Sir Kay gasped. "It's gone!"

Arthur turned quite pale with horror. It was a squire's job to make sure that a knight was properly equipped. "We must have left it at the lodging house we stayed at last night," he groaned. "Don't worry, Kay. I'll dash back and fetch it." Before anyone could argue, Arthur had wheeled his horse around and was galloping at full tilt back down the road. There wasn't a second to lose.

But when Arthur arrived back at the lodging house, there wasn't a sign of Sir Kay's sword anywhere. Arthur raced his horse back to the city wondering how on earth he was going to break the bad news to his brother. He was very nearly at the jousting field when he galloped past the cathedral courtyard and saw the sword sticking out of the magical anvil on the stone. Arthur reined in his panting horse at once and looked all around him. There was no one about; everyone was at the jousting competition. It certainly didn't look as though the sword would be missed if he borrowed it for a while. "I promise I'll bring it back later," Arthur muttered out loud to no one in particular. He dashed over the snow, jumped up onto the stone and grasped the sword. It slid out of the anvil as easily as a needle pulls through cloth. "Gadzooks!" Arthur breathed, as he gazed at the mighty, jewelled blade in his hands. "This is the most magnificent weapon I have ever seen!" Then he remembered that the competition was about to begin. He sprinted back to his horse, leapt into the saddle, and arrived at the jousting field just as the fanfares were being trumpeted.

Sir Kay was astonished at the superb weapon that his younger brother handed him. He and his father had just heard all about the mysterious anvil from the other knights at the jousting competition, and he realized at once where the strange sword must have come from. "See, father!" he cried over the crowds, brandishing the sword over his head. "I must be the new king of the Britons!"

Sir Ector came running at once and gasped at the magnificent weapon in Kay's hands. "How have you got this?" he demanded.

Kay's face fell. "Arthur brought it to me," he mumbled.

Sir Ector's face was grave. "Who pulled this out of the stone and gave it to you?" he quizzed Arthur.

"N-n-o one," stammered Arthur. Quite a few people had gathered around by now and suddenly he felt very nervous. "I pulled it out of the stone myself. I was going to put it back when Kay had finished with it, honest!"

Sir Ector led Arthur back to the cathedral and into the courtyard, with a huge and excited crowd following hot on their heels. "Put the sword back where you found it, son," he told Arthur.

"All right," shrugged Arthur. He climbed onto the stone and thrust the sword back into the anvil.

First, Sir Ector himself tried to pull it out. Then Sir Kay heaved at it with all his might. The sword didn't budge an inch.

"Now show us how you did it, son," said Sir Ector, his voice trembling slightly.

Everyone held their breath as Arthur stepped up to the anvil. As he pulled the sword out effortlessly, the cheer that went up could be heard all over the capital city and beyond.

And that is how a young boy called Arthur, who wasn't even a knight, was crowned king of the Britons and eventually became the greatest of all the heroes who ever lived in the Celtic lands.

The Princess and the Pea

By Hans Christian Andersen

The prince was very fed up. Everyone in the court, from his father, the king, down to the smallest page, seemed to think it was time he was married. Now the prince would have been very happy to get married, but he did insist that his bride be a princess, a real true and proper princess. He had travelled the land and met plenty of nice girls who said they were princesses, but none, it seemed to him, were really true and proper princesses. Either their manners were not quite exquisite enough, or their feet were much too big. So he sat in the palace, reading dusty old history books and getting very glum.

One night, there was the most terrible storm.

Rain was lashing down, and thunder and lightning rolled and flashed round the palace. The wind kept blowing out the candles, and everyone huddled closer to the fire. Suddenly there was a great peal from the huge front door bell.

And there, absolutely dripping wet, stood a princess. Well, she said she was a princess, but never did anyone look less like a princess. Her hair was plastered to her head, her dress was wringing wet and her silk shoes were covered in mud. She was quite alone, without even the smallest maid, and just where had she come from? But she kept insisting she was a princess.

We will see about that, thought the queen. While the dripping girl sat sipping a mug of warm milk and honey, the queen went to supervise the making of the bed in the second-best spare bedroom. She didn't think it necessary to put their late night visitor in the best spare bedroom, after all she might only be a common or garden duchess. The queen told the maids to take all the bedclothes and the mattress off the bed. Then she placed one single pea right on the middle of the bedstead. Next the maids piled twenty mattresses on top of the pea, and then twenty feather quilts on top of the mattresses. And so the girl was left for the night.

In the morning, the queen swept into the bedroom in her dressing gown and asked the girl how she had slept.

"I didn't sleep a wink all night." said the girl. "There was a great, hard lump in the middle of the bed. It was quite dreadful. I am sure I am black and blue all over!"

Now everyone knew she really must be a princess, for only a real princess could be as soft-skinned as that. The prince was delighted, and insisted they got married at once, and they lived very happily ever after. They always slept in very soft beds, and the pea was placed in the museum, where it probably still is today.

The Twelve Dancing Princesses

By the Brothers Grimm

The king was very puzzled. He had twelve daughters, each one as beautiful as the moon and the stars, and he loved them above all the riches in his kingdom. But every morning the princesses would appear yawning and bleary-eyed, and with their shoes quite worn through. Every evening the king would kiss them good night and lock the door behind him. So how did they get out? And where did they go?

Buying new shoes every day was costing him a fortune so the king determined to solve the mystery. The court messenger was sent to all four corners of the kingdom to issue the king's proclamation that he would give the hand of one of his daughters in marriage to any man who could discover the secret. But should he fail after three nights he would be banished forever.

Needless to say there were plenty of young men willing to risk banishment to win such a prize. But they soon found the princesses were too clever by half. Before they realized it, morning had come and there were the sleepy princesses and twelve pairs of worn-out shoes.

Now into the kingdom at this time there wandered a penniless soldier who decided to try his luck when an old woman came slowly down the dusty road. The young man offered her some of his bread and cheese, and as they sat together the old woman asked where he was bound. When he explained, she said, "You must not drink the mead those princesses offer you, for it is drugged. Pretend to be asleep, and you shall see what you shall see. This may help you," and the old woman handed him a cloak.

"Whenever you wear this you will be invisible. Use it well!" and the old woman disappeared. "Well, perhaps I will succeed now I have magic on my side," murmured the young man as he set off for the palace.

The young man bowed deeply to the king and smiled at all the princesses. He ate a hearty supper but when a princess gave him a goblet of mead he only pretended to drink it. Then he yawned loudly and let his head droop as if he had fallen asleep.

The butler and the first footman dumped the young man onto the bed placed across the door of the princesses' bedchamber. He cautiously opened one eye and gazed around the room. The princesses were putting on gorgeous velvet dresses and the brand new jewelled slippers that the shoemaker had only delivered a few hours earlier. The eldest princess clapped her hands three times.

A trap door opened up in the floor and they all swiftly descended down a steeply curving staircase. The young man flung the magic cloak round his shoulders and rushed after them.

He found himself in a wondrous garden where the trees were covered in rich jewels, sparkling in candlelight. Musicians played whirling tunes and he saw all the princesses dancing with the most handsome princes. The young man was spellbound, but he managed to keep his wits about him. He broke off a branch from one of the jewelled trees and hid it under his cloak. Then he ran back and lay down on his bed.

It was with a weary voice that the king asked the young man at breakfast if he had found out where the princesses went. The king sat up quickly when the young man told his tale and produced the branch from the tree. The king was delighted and the young man chose the youngest sister for his bride. And they all lived happily ever after.

The Frog Prince

By the Brothers Grimm

Once upon a time, there lived a very spoilt princess who never seemed content. The more she had, the more she wanted. And she just would not do as she was told.

One day she took her golden ball out into the woods. She threw it high up into the sky once, twice, but the third time it slipped from her hands and, with a great splash, it fell down, down into a deep well. The princess stamped her foot and yelled, but this did not help. So she kicked the side of the well and a large frog plopped out.

"Ugh!" said the princess. "A horrible slimy frog," but the frog didn't move. Instead, it said, "What are you making such a fuss about?"

A talking frog! For a moment the princess was speechless, but then she looked down her nose and said, "If you must know, my golden ball has fallen down this well, and I want it back."

With a sudden leap, the frog disappeared down the well. In the wink of an eye, it was back with the golden ball.

The princess went to snatch it up, but the frog put a wet foot rather firmly on it and said,

"Hasn't anyone taught you any manners? I have a special request to make."

The princess looked at the frog in astonishment. No one ever dared talk to her like that. She glared at the frog and said crossly, "May I have my ball back, please, and what is your special request?"

The frog bent closer to the princess. "I want to come and live with you in the palace and eat off your plate and sleep on your pillow, please."

The princess looked horrified, but she was sure a promise to a frog wouldn't count so she said, "Of course you can," and grabbed her ball from frog and ran back to the palace very quickly.

That night at supper the royal family heard a strange voice calling, "Princess, where are you?" and in hopped the frog.

The queen fainted. The king frowned.

"Do you know this frog, princess?" he asked.

"Oh bother!" said the princess again, but she had to tell her father what had happened. He insisted the princess keep her promise.

The frog ate very little, the princess even less. And when it was time to go to bed, the king just looked very sternly at the princess who was trying to sneak off on her own. She picked the frog up by one leg, and when she reached her great four-poster bed, she plonked the frog down in the farthest corner. She did not sleep a wink all night.

The next evening, the frog was back. Supper was a quiet affair. The queen stayed in her room, the king read the newspaper, and the princess tried not to look at the frog. Bedtime came, and once again the frog and the princess slept at opposite ends of the bed.

The third evening, the princess was terribly hungry so she just pretended the frog was not there and ate everything that was placed in front of her. When it came to bedtime, she was so exhausted that she fell in a deep sleep.

The next morning when she woke up, she felt much better for her good sleep until she remembered the frog. But it was nowhere to be seen.

At the foot of the bed, however, there stood a handsome young man in a green velvet suit.

"Hello, princess," he said. "I was the frog who rescued your golden ball. I was bewitched by a fairy who said I was rude and spoilt. The spell could only be broken by someone equally rude being nice to me."

The princess was speechless. The king was most impressed with the man's manners, and the queen liked his fine suit. Everyone liked the fact that the princess had become much nicer and before long, the princess and the young man were married.